the light in me sees the light in you

LORI NICHOLS

Nancy Paulsen Books

For Rachel Estes—who sees the light in everyone.
And in loving memory of Lisa Gustafson, Glenn Feldman,
Bob and Barbara Nichols, Greg McKendry, and Linda Kraeger,
whose light will never stop shining.

Nancy Paulsen Books
An imprint of Penguin Random House LLC, New York

Visit us online at penguinrandomhouse.com

Library of Congress Cataloging-in-Publication Data is available.

Manufactured in China by RR Donnelley Asia Printing Solutions Ltd.
ISBN 9780399544859
1 3 5 7 9 10 8 6 4 2

Design by Marikka Tamura
Text set in Finch Frame 3
The illustrations for this book were rendered in watercolor, colored pencil, collage, and digital techniques.

It happened one day.
First I heard you.

Then I saw you.

The light in me saw the light in you.

And we became friends.

We both liked listening
to the wind sing . . .

looking at clouds . . .

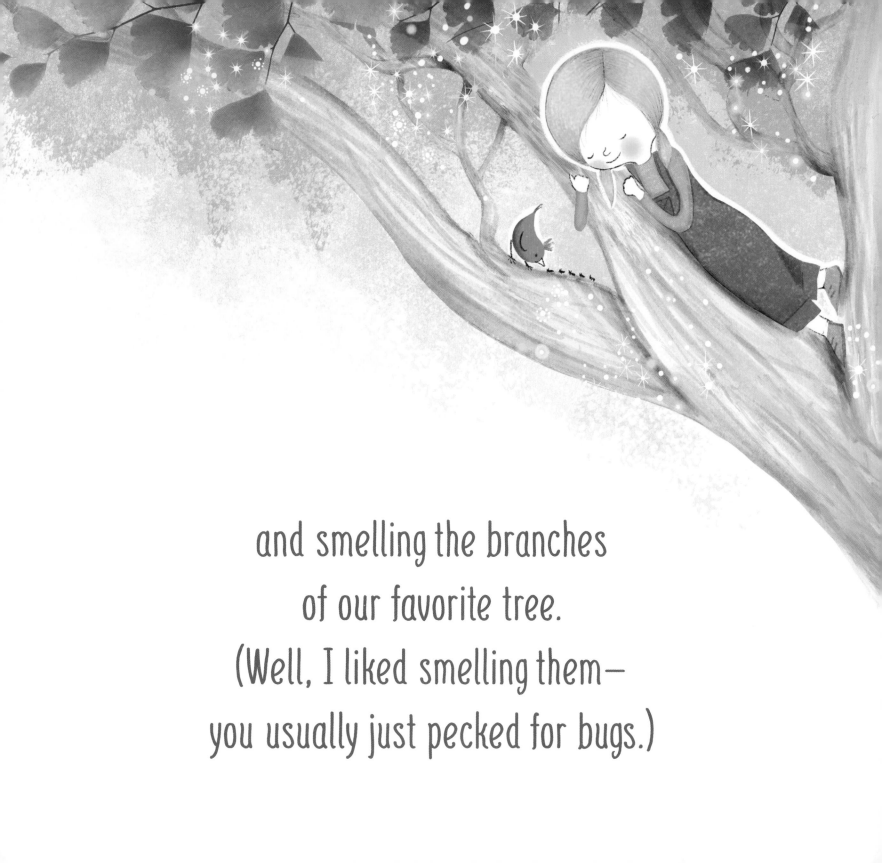

and smelling the branches
of our favorite tree.
(Well, I liked smelling them—
you usually just pecked for bugs.)

We both loved splashing in puddles
and the feel of raindrops on our heads.

I liked sharing my food with you.

You tried to share yours with me.
(Maybe I will learn to like worms someday.)

And we both loved flying—

well, I'm still learning.

Some days we wanted to be alone—
together.

But one day . . .

I listened for you,
but couldn't hear you.

I looked for you,
but couldn't see you.

Without you, being alone

felt too lonely.

Then one night you visited me in my dreams.
I felt your light . . .

and you finally taught me how to fly.

Now I hear you in the wind.

I see you in the clouds.

I remember you in the rain.

The light in you will always be part of the light in me.